Marthe J

The Invisible Day

illustrated by **Abby Carter**

SCHOLASTIC INC.

New York Toronto London Auckland Sydney
Mexico City New Delhi Hong Kong

ISBN 0-439-15575-4

Text copyright © 1997 by Marthe Jocelyn.
Illustrations copyright © 1997 by Abby Carter. All rights reserved.
Published by Scholastic Inc., 555 Broadway, New York, NY 10012,
by arrangement with Dutton Children's Books,
a division of Penguin Books USA Inc.
SCHOLASTIC and associated logos are trademarks
and/or registered trademarks of Scholastic Inc.

12 11 10 9 8 7 6 5 4 3 2 1   9/9 0 1 2 3 4/0

Printed in the U.S.A.   40

First Scholastic printing, September 1999

Designed by Semadar Megged

CONTENTS

THE INVISIBLE DAY

1 • Stuck Like Glue

Even though I am almost eleven years old, my mother is stuck to me like glue.

It seems like kids everywhere else in the world are walking to school alone, scooting down to the corner store for a pack of gum, or going over to a friend's house after supper for a game of basketball. But I live in New York! Home of muggers, dive-bombing pigeons, the subway, and people who talk to hydrants. I've noticed that grown-ups are delighted to list the countless dangers. And one of these days, I'm going to have to look after myself out there in the wilds.

When I read books about kids my age, I am amazed at how little their mothers have to do with their lives. They are either dead, or busy doctors, or famous actresses who have convenient world tours whenever the kid has an adventure. The fathers are either dead, or distracted professors, or away at sea for months at a time.

My father doesn't live with us anymore, but my mother is with me every single minute of every single day of my life. We live in a loft, which is like an apartment except it's all open. My mom has a real room with a door, but the rest is just a big, huge space divided by half walls and screens.

My sister, Jane, and I have to share the area next to the windows that look out on Broadway. This is not the Broadway with theaters and sparkly lights and people in tuxedos smoking cigars. This is the Broadway where trucks roar past all night long. So if Jane doesn't keep me awake by grinding her teeth, there are horns honking and brakes screeching.

My only personal territory is the top bunk. I don't bother to keep a diary because I have no private life to record.

My mother has the one job guaranteed to keep us in her sight: She is the librarian at our school and has not missed a day of work since she started the job four years ago. You would think that by the weekend, she'd be ready for a rest. But, even though we do get to sleep in, plus watch cartoons, we also have to have a weekly Family Excursion, and that means Together.

So, on the second Sunday in April, my mother decided to take us to Central Park for the first picnic of the spring. Central Park is the biggest collection of grass and trees in New York City and, since we don't have a backyard, we like to go there. We usually start at the bottom of the park, at Fifty-ninth Street. We walk past the artists who draw dopey chalk portraits of tourists and then go along the path that leads to the zoo.

We only go *into* the zoo about twice a year,

usually on an icy Sunday in February when going to the tropical house is like a vacation in
Brazil. It's like being inside a kettle just after the
tea is made. Most often, we don't pay to go in;
we just hang over the fence and watch the seals
being fed.

"Why do they like fish so much?" asked
Jane.

"Because they live in the ocean, and that's
the only thing they can get their hands on," I
told her.

"You mean their flippers on," she said.

We watched the trainer tossing slippery silver bodies into the air and the seals craning
their necks just slightly to make the catch.

"Do you think they like French fries?" asked
Jane.

"They would probably throw up if they had
French fries," said my mother.

"Oh, let's try it next time," said Jane to me.
"I want to see what seal throw-up looks like."

"That's gross, Jane," I said, giving her the
tiniest push. She shoved me back, hard. I

stepped on her toe, just on the edge, and she screamed as though I had cut off her foot with an axe and fed it to the seals.

My mother got mad and, of course, took Jane's side and said I had to wait at the bottom of the first rock until Jane climbed ahead. She knew that would really bug me.

The best part of Central Park is the way huge rocks burst out of the ground like kid-size mountains. Some of them are covered in lichen or have trees growing out of the cracks. Some of them are just solid gray lumps, waiting to be scaled by heroic explorers. This is one of my favorite activities.

I sat with my back to my horrible mother and kicked at weeds. There was a broken bottle and a lot of ants crawling over sludge that used to be orange soda. I threw pebbles at a boulder, trying to make them land on the mossy patch on the top. I looked at my watch to see how many seconds had passed. I examined the sky, trying to see sideways how far Jane had climbed without actually looking in her direction. She had not gotten very far because she really needs me to be the leader on these expeditions. I could tell she was torn between wanting to show that she could climb by herself and being too scared to even try. I stood up and kicked some more weeds.

And that's when I saw the bag.

2 • *In the Bag*

It was lying just behind the boulder, mostly hidden by the tall grass. It was made of pink quilted satin, printed with green flowers, which is why it stayed hidden. It was about the size of a paperback book. It must have dropped out of someone's purse. I stood looking at it, not even bending over, thinking hard and fast.

I looked around. All the way around. I turned a slow, casual circle to check in all directions. There were a boyfriend and girlfriend on a bench in the middle of a sloppy kiss. There was a man with a dog walking away down the path. No one was watching me.

My mother was watching Jane with a parental glow. Jane was inching up the rock face and concentrating hard. I sat on the boulder so that my foot touched the bag and gave it a little nudge. It was heavy. I slid my backpack off and put it on the ground. I leaned over to adjust a buckle and deftly popped the bag inside.

I had to open my jacket. I was sweating under my arms. I never stole anything before. But this wasn't really stealing. Finders keepers, right?

Another swift glance at the family confirmed success. I was the proud owner of a secret.

I shouldered my pack and strolled over to watch Jane climb. She was almost at the top and had a big grin on her face.

"I'd just like to say I'm sorry for being a bully, even though I wasn't really, but I certainly did not mean to harm Jane in any way."

My mother's mouth actually gaped open.

"I'll be going now," I added, before there could be any discussion.

I lunged at the rock and climbed fast. My backpack was going to stay on my back, like a koala baby, for the rest of the day.

Jane stuck out her tongue when I caught up with her, but I was way past fighting with a six-year-old.

"Hey, Jane! You did a great climb!"

She wrinkled her nose in suspicion.

"I mean it. Plus look down there." I pointed to the couple on the bench. "Smooch Alert! Smooch Alert!"

She collapsed with glee. I had won back her heart.

We climbed rocks until Jane skinned her

shin. We listened to a folk singer beside the boat pond, who made my mother's face go all moony. It seemed like I could feel the little bag the whole time, burning like a hot-water bottle in the middle of my back.

We ate our lunch near the statue of Alice in Wonderland. We had peanut butter and jelly on bagels and cut-up melon and granola bars.

I thought I had a chance to look at my prize while my mother went to watch Jane climb Alice, but Jane just perched on one of the bronze toadstools, and my mother came right back to sit with me. My fingers lay inside my backpack, quietly stroking the satin.

We got ice cream from the man with one leg. We watched the miniature sailboats scud across the boat pond by remote control. When we finally got out of the park, my mother spent about seven hours looking at used books in the bookstalls on Fifth Avenue. She didn't buy anything.

Hidden treasure was just a block away when we dragged our feet up the stairs of the subway station onto our very own street corner. So it was extra annoying that we bumped right into our neighbors, Sarah and Joe and their baby, Tucker, and got invited over for pizza.

More waiting. When the pizza got there, I ate two slices in four minutes.

"Mom," I whispered. "Can we go home now?"

"In a few minutes, honey."

"Really a few? Or a mother's idea of a few?"

She raised her eyebrow in that mad-in-front-of-company way.

"It's just that it's a school night, Mom. Shouldn't we be getting to bed?"

She felt my forehead, like I might have a fever. And then she said yes to more wine.

It was way past dark when we got back to our loft. I could tell Mom wanted to hustle us through the pajama–teeth–story routine, but I went into the bathroom and closed the door. I could not wait one more minute to have a look in the bag.

The zipper stuck a little when I pulled on it,

but I held my breath and got it open without jamming.

Inside, it looked almost like my mother's makeup pouch, but really used. There were three little black jars with pearly tops and a plastic case with three colors of eye shadow and a few Q-tips. The lid of the compact was cracked. There was a box of miniature soap, two lipsticks, and a sewing kit with *The Plaza Hotel* stamped on the side. There was also a bus pass and a Dr. Dingo's Science Club membership card for somebody named Jody Greengard.

I opened one of the lipstick cases and rotated the bottom. It was bright coral.

"Billie?" my mother called. "Is everything all right in there?"

"I'll be out in a minute, Mom."

"Are you cleaning the bathtub with your tongue, by any chance?"

"Mom!"

"Jane has to pee, honey; could you hurry up?"

I stuffed the bag back into my pack and marched out of the bathroom. Jane crashed past me to the toilet.

"I'll hang this up for you while you get into your jammies," said my mother, scooping the pack from my shoulder.

"Uh, no, no, I'll do it." I grabbed toward my treasure.

"Billie Stoner, not one more word. Get ready for bed."

I lay in bed, twitching. I could hear my mother brush her teeth and gargle a long gargle. I heard her drawers open and close and then the soft flap of her duvet.

Go to sleep. I was sending brain signals. I heard the click of the remote control and a burst of TV sound before she turned down the volume and watched the news, just to torture me.

I was trying to remember how many different things there were in the bag, counting them in my head. Trucks rattled by outside. Finally, the TV went off and her light went out. I practiced breathing like a burglar. I slowly counted to three hundred and then climbed down my ladder. I took eight steps. The floor creaked like in a haunted house. I took three more steps.

Suddenly the light flashed on and my heart jumped out of my ears. My mother stood in the doorway to her room with her eyebrows squeezed together.

"I'm thirsty."

She glared. I hustled over to the sink and got a quick drink. I almost ran back to bed. My mother just stood there.

My bag might as well be in jail. I put a pillow over my head and begged for sleep.

3 • *The Routine*

My mother wakes us up in the morning, singing a cheery little song about greeting the sun. Jane likes it, but I think it is as annoying as the kitchen timer.

I slept through it this time, and she had to shake me awake. As soon as I was conscious, I had one goal in mind: Get alone with the bag.

Monday is early chorus rehearsal. We have to be there by 8:15. I dragged on my jeans and purple sweatshirt in two minutes and combed my hair in two seconds. I snatched my bagel from the counter to eat on the way.

I took my backpack from its hook and quickly checked inside. Then I slid it onto my shoulders like an enchanted cloak, ready for anything.

"Come on, you guys!" I was already in the elevator while Jane was still nibbling her three bites of Cheerios. And she couldn't just put

on a jacket. She had to add a scarf and a bandanna and a purse full of rubber mice.

"Jane, that's enough. You are a fashion disaster!" Even my mother was impatient today. She was taking a group of second-graders to the Central Library this morning. The idea is to introduce them to a real library, but mostly they want to climb on the giant stone lions beside the steps on Fifth Avenue.

Finally, we headed out into the world. Getting to school with Jane is like taking a pet snail for a walk. And we have to poke along at her pace because my mother goes crazy if I go even half a block ahead on the street. What if an out-of-control taxi jumps the curb and plows me over? What if a bad guy in a helicopter swoops down and kidnaps me? What if an earthquake cracks the sidewalk and she has to watch me being swallowed? You get the idea.

My best friend, Hubert, was already in the music room when we got there. He was leaning against the piano, chewing gum and looking through our favorite book, *The Human Body.* It has pictures of people with their skin peeled off, showing veins and muscles and eyeballs. It also has chapters on nasty diseases and babies being born.

Hubert is the one person on earth who has a name that is worse than mine. My name is Isobel. Isobel! In this day and age! *What* were they thinking? According to my mother, she had a great-great-aunt who was very, very rich, and when she was on her deathbed, she said if the firstborn was named after her, she would bequeath a fortune to the blessed infant.

"So where's my fortune?" I ask.

"Her name was Rose," she tells me.

Luckily, I called myself Iz-bill as soon as I could talk. And that turned into Billie. So that's what I'm really called.

But poor Hubert. He is Chinese, and he claims that when his parents arrived in New York with their brand-new baby, a helpful government official with five daughters convinced them to give him his own "all-American" name, knowing it would be the last kid ever called Hubert.

My mother was gabbing to Hubert's mother and Sam's dad. I gave her my quality half smile, and she blew me a kiss. I ducked. She winked and went off happily toward the library stairs, leaving me to my own life for a few hours.

"Hubert," I called from across the room. "I have something so important to tell you."

4 • *Going, Going, Gone*

Hey, Bertie!" As usual, seeing us together, Alyssa couldn't miss the chance to be mean.

"I said, Hey, Bertie!" she hooted, knocking his arm so that the book slammed to the floor. I stared at her coldly. Hubert's problem is that he doesn't stand up for himself. He's too polite. He doesn't even like to talk out loud to more than one person.

"Hey, Bertie. Did anyone ever tell you that your hair looks like a lawn that someone mowed in the wrong direction?" Hubert rolled his lips around and stood on one leg. I think his hair is cute. It stands straight up and looks like the glossy pelt of a panther you'd like to pat.

"Alyssa," I snarl, "did anyone ever tell you that your face looks like oww!" Hubert kicked me. He was reminding me not to stoop to her level, as tempting as it might be.

"Hey, Bertie, good thing you brought your baby-sitter along. Too bad she's got breath like a garbage dump."

"At least I don't sing like a seal." I had to have the last word, even though she actually sounds like a real singer, all clear and trembly.

She smirked and turned away to look for other victims, flicking her perfect braid over her shoulder.

"What did you want to tell me?" Hubert retrieved the book from the floor. I signaled that Alyssa was lurking too nearby. He caught on quickly. That's why I like him.

"Um, did you choose your country?" He changed the subject. He was talking about the Small World Project, which Ms. McPhee had been explaining on Friday. Each of us had to choose a country and do research to find out all about it and then pretend to be from there and tell the rest of the class everything we'd learned. We were supposed to be improving our research skills—using the encyclopedia and other information sources.

"Yeah, I got a really cool idea. I chose Liechtenstein because it's the smallest country in the world and it has a population that is way smaller than New York City and I thought I could use that for a comparison."

"Hey, and mine has the biggest population in the world! That's cool!"

Everybody knew that Hubert was going to do China.

Mr. Belenky strode into the music room and immediately tapped his baton against a music stand.

"Places, please."

I had one second to decide.

"Come along, sopranos, tidy up that row."

"Hubert," I whispered, "I'm going to the bathroom."

I dashed for the door while Mr. Belenky fumbled with the song sheets. I suddenly felt hot all over my head. I went straight to the girls' room at the end of the lower hallway.

One tap was dripping, a steady *plink, plink, plink.* Otherwise, it was completely quiet.

I stood between the two sinks and took the

little bag out of my pack. The zipper stuck again but I teased it open. I unscrewed the lid of the first pearly pot. Inside was a pale green cream that smelled like cucumbers too long in the sun. The next jar held a buttery-colored lotion that smelled like pudding. The compact sprang open when I touched the gold clasp. The mirror inside the lid was shaped like a heart. The powder in the shallow dish was loose and shimmery.

I stirred it a bit with my fingertip and patted some onto my nose. It was soft and thick, like crushed chalk or cocoa powder. I rubbed more on my cheeks and arms. It had the faint smell of stale toffee. I felt, not exactly a tingle, but

a warming. For a moment, it made my skin gleam.

Then, even though it's impossible, I seemed to get fuzzy, like a photograph out of focus. And then, before my very own eyes, I began to disappear!

It was the strangest feeling I've ever had, watching myself fade away to nothing. Even when I was gone, I could see. I mean, my eyes still worked so I could look in the mirror, but it was the toilet stalls I was looking at. The ugly green painted doors, the gray tiled walls, and the paper towel dispenser. I was just not there anymore!

"This," I said aloud, "is really weird." I could talk and I could hear!

"This is as weird as it can be." My voice sounded hollow, but maybe it always sounds that way in the bathroom and had nothing to do with my body disappearing.

I stared into the mirror. I tried to swallow. What was I supposed to do now? Walk into chorus practice and start singing? Go out and confess? "Uh, yeah, I found this bag and kept it for myself. I used the stuff inside and now, well, now I'm gone!" I imagined the look on my mother's face. I decided to keep thinking.

Maybe if I washed it off?

It was a relief that I could grasp and turn the tap without visible fingers. I could feel the water splashing over my hands and face, but nothing happened. Except that now I had drippy hands and a wet face.

Suddenly I heard voices outside the door. And a giggle that could only be Alyssa's. I scooped up the powder and the other jars in half a second and nearly screamed when they vanished at my touch. I dropped them into my pack like burning matches. They reappeared instantly.

The bathroom door swung open. Without thinking, I dove for cover in one of the toilet stalls, just as Alyssa burst in with Sarah right behind her.

I had left my backpack on the floor beside the sink.

5 • *Telling Hubert*

I know she's in here," said Alyssa in her bossy way. "I saw her go in. Billie! Billie? Aha!" She had spotted my pack.

"Her pack is here," said Sarah helpfully. "So she must be, too."

I was an ice statue, cold with fear and as still as a toilet. I clenched my hands and closed my eyes, waiting for Alyssa to see my feet.

Then I almost choked, trying to hold in a laugh. I was invisible!

Alyssa poked her nose under the stall door, trying to catch me balancing on the toilet seat, but she looked right through me. I stuck out my tongue at her upside-down face.

"She's not here." I could hear her disappointment. "How did she get out? Come on, Sarah, let's get her in trouble. She's late for chorus."

"She's probably *in* chorus, Alyssa," I heard

Sarah grumble. "We're the ones who are late."

Sarah is new this year. Her family just moved here from Wisconsin. Alyssa snatched her up instantly so she would have a slave-girl. So now nobody else really hangs out with her. Other than being friends with Alyssa, her only mistake is that she hasn't realized yet that fifth-graders in New York City do not wear pink. She'll catch on.

"Maybe I won't snitch just yet," said Alyssa. "But I'm taking this hostage."

Her shiny boots clattered out the door, with Sarah trailing.

I knew without looking that she had my backpack.

I had to get Hubert right away. I glanced in the mirror to check that I still wasn't there. I left the bathroom and tiptoed down the hall to the music room. There he was, in the alto section, gazing up at Mr. Belenky like a choirboy.

Sarah's head was bowed and Alyssa's cheeks were bright pink so I knew they'd gotten the evil eye. Too bad I missed it. Lucky for me, Mr. Belenky would never stop a song to listen to Alyssa. He just glares if you're late and usually glares at the parents, too, assuming it's their fault. My pack was between Alyssa's feet at the end of the second row.

I realized I would have to think about my approach. It would be too easy to scare the wits out of Hubert. And this kind of thing just doesn't happen every day.

I retreated to the hallway. Under the bulletin

board was a stack of flyers for the middle school play. I scribbled on the back of one of them.

Hubert! Emergency!
Before class, go to boys' bathroom,
2nd floor. Billie.

I hadn't really noticed before how bathrooms were the only place where a kid can be alone. I chose that one because it's a single, with a lock on the main door.

I folded the note twice and put it on the upper shelf of Hubert's cubbie, where I knew he would find it soon, wrapped around his stash of banana gum.

It had been only ten minutes according to my Flik-Flak watch but, crouched next to the sink, I got a little stiff. I was trying not to worry about my predicament. It could even be fun, eavesdropping and going places where maybe I shouldn't be.

Mostly, I just kept hoping that no one would come in to use the toilet or that other weird piece of plumbing. Finally, I heard Hubert's triple knock, and I triple-knocked back. He opened the door and looked astounded at the empty room.

"Hubert," I whispered, "it's okay; come in; I'm invisible."

He was not reassured. His face slid into a pudding of worry, and I could almost feel his hand sweating on the doorknob.

"Hubert, I promise, it's okay. Please come in before anyone sees you standing there like a dodo-bird. I need your help."

He stepped in automatically and closed the door behind him.

"Where are you?" Hubert's eyes were roaming around the room.

"I'm over here, you idiot! Look at me!" I grabbed his hand and he gasped, but I had his attention in more or less the right direction.

"Uh, does your mother know about this?"

"What do you think?"

"You're in trouble, Billie. Plus, you're in the boys' bathroom."

"Duh."

We were quiet for a minute.

"Lucky for you, Ms. McPhee is sick today. We have a substitute, with purple frames on her glasses. Talk about ugly!" He wiped his face. Enough chitchat.

"What happened?" He perched on the toilet. "This is really creepy, Billie."

"I was trying to tell you before chorus. I found a little bag in Central Park and inside were all these little jars full of cream and powder and stuff and I didn't realize they were magic and . . ." I couldn't even show him! "I can't even show you because Alyssa stole my backpack with all the stuff inside. You have to help me get it back."

"From Alyssa?"

"Yeah, from Alyssa. Maybe you could be invisible with me!"

He perked up immediately.

"But we have to get my pack. And we have to swipe the attendance sheet when it goes down to the office and check off our names. It's so cool that McPhee is sick. The sub won't know my mother."

Hubert's head started to shake back and forth in double time.

"I don't think so, Billie. This is maybe not such a good idea."

"Hubert, it's our big chance. We can go outside and see the world and the world can't see us. Hubert, come on!"

"Billie, you're dreaming. You—"

There was a knock on the door. We froze.

6 • Walking Tall

Hubert? This is Ms. Maloney." It was a perky voice. "Are you okay?"

"The substitute," hissed Hubert.

I poked him.

"Uh, yes, ma'am," he stuttered.

"Well, then. Get a move on. You should be preparing for the math quiz."

"Flush the toilet," I whispered. He flushed the toilet.

"Turn on the taps." He turned on the taps.

"What are you going to do, Billie?" He was really washing his hands.

I knew what I was going to do.

He reached for the paper towel. I had to keep dodging him.

"I'm going to go out, Hubert. Outside, by myself. Just for a little while. I'll meet you back here in an hour. And you have to get my pack from Alyssa. That's your mission. And cover for me."

There was another knock.

"I'll be okay," I whispered. "You better go."

I watched him walk down the hall behind the substitute. He kept looking back. He even lifted his fingers in a goofy little wave. I tore off a piece of paper towel and let it float to the floor so he'd know I was there.

Ms. Shephard, our door dragon, was sitting in her cubicle in the front hall, with her glasses shoved up on her forehead. She always wears some junky piece of collage jewelry that her kid made.

The pink attendance sheets were in a stack on the ledge right in front of her. I waved my hand in her face. She didn't flinch.

The phone rang. Ms. Shephard turned toward the switchboard, and I gently thumbed the top corners of the pages, looking for Ms. McPhee's class. Just as the swivel chair swung back, I found the right page and slid it to the ground. The paper had to lie on the floor so that I could see it to find my name. I stood up to swipe a pencil and crouched down again. I made a tiny check, just like the ones Ms. Maloney had done. When the phone rang again, I put the page back. Easy as pie.

I put my fingers into my ears, stuck out my tongue at Ms. Shephard, and wiggled like Jane doing a belly dance. No reaction.

Oh, boy, this was going to be fun!

As soon as I stepped outside the school, though, I took a big breath. It was the first time in my life that I had been on the street all by myself. Not exactly by myself, of course. I guess if those half million other people could have seen me, they wouldn't have bumped into me so much.

I concentrated on walking tall with my shoulders back. That's what my mother says is the best way to seem confident. I realized that no one could see me, but I kept on doing it anyway, just to fool myself.

I went along Bleecker Street because it was the most familiar. I had walked this block on the way to school with Jane and my mom, and it had been just regular. The deli, the funeral parlor, the Japanese restaurant never open till noon, the watch repair, the bagel shop: just regular.

Now it seemed about to explode with adventure, as if all the doorways might burst open together and let a stampede of clowns tumble into the street. Or a flock of giant larks might perch on the water towers and douse the air with a joyous song. It seemed possible.

I was just walking along, but it seemed like a dramatic adventure.

I was suddenly starving. My breakfast bagel

was a long time ago. I stopped outside a fruit market called City Eden. I had a dollar bill and three nickels in my pocket, but I figured that money magically appearing and my voice coming out of thin air could only cause trouble. I would just have to steal.

I slipped into the store right behind a man with an orange beard and his little boy. The kid was smaller than Jane.

"Daddy! Daddy! Daddy! I want, I want Sunshine crackers, I said, Daddy, I want Sunshine crackers, Daddy, Daddy, I want Sunshine crackers!"

"Ben, please use your regular voice. I don't understand when you whine."

This brat was the perfect cover, even if I hadn't been invisible. He was so noisy that the clerk stared at him in disgust. She didn't notice the sudden gap in the row of bananas or the bag of Doritos that I scooped from the rack right under her elbow.

Out on the street again, my neck was warm with triumph. I started to think about the wide

range of possibilities for an invisible thief. F A O
Schwarz! Barnes & Noble! The candy depart-
ment of Dean & Deluca! I could have anything I
wanted!

I ate the banana and tossed the peel toward
the wire garbage basket on the corner. Swish.
Only Ben saw the miracle.

"Daddy, Daddy, Daddy, a flying banana peel,
Daddy, look, I seed, I seed a banana . . ."

"Ben, slow down. If you talk in your regular
voice, I might . . ."

I walked in the opposite direction, toward SoHo. I ate my tortilla chips with what my mom calls gusto. I would have whistled, but my mouth was full. At Houston Street I stopped with a lurch.

I know it sounds goofy, but I had never crossed such a big street alone.

"This is a tricky corner," said a man next to me. I looked down to see if the spell had worn off. It hadn't.

"Too many cars making the right-hand turn."

I glanced around, wondering who he was talking to.

"Would you guide me across?" Oh, duh, I thought. He was holding a white cane! I realized that, because he was blind, his hearing was extra sensitive. He knew I was there when nobody else did.

"Hello!" he said sharply. "Would you guide me across the street?"

"Of course, sir," I piped up, "certainly, sir!" I brushed the Dorito dust off my fingers and put my hand under his arm. When the light changed, we stepped into the road. The drivers waiting to turn saw a blind man tapping his way through traffic. We crossed the street safely.

"Thank you; I'm fine from here," he said when we got to the other side. A hot-dog vendor looked sideways at him as he waved his cane at me and marched off.

7 • *Magic Movie Moments*

There were ten huge silver trucks parked on Prince Street, a sure sign that a movie was being made. The sidewalk was crisscrossed with black, snaky cords. Blazing white lights shone down on the Vesuvio Bakery. Tony de Angelo, the real-life baker, was hovering off to one side.

Every week, it seems, there is another movie or TV show being shot in our neighborhood. It's partly because of our unusual buildings. They are covered with stone decorations, like chunky old birthday cakes. The roof lines and window frames are covered with angels and lions and curlicues, all made of stone. You can always recognize tourists in New York, my mom says, because they walk along gaping upward. Well, I live here and I think it's cool, too.

The bakery is what my mom calls quaint. It looks about a hundred years old, with cracking green paint and a window lined with paper, full of fancy breads.

Right now there were four husky men trying to aim a spotlight through the window at just the right angle. There was an actor standing inside, dressed like a storybook baker, with a white hat and floury apron. I guess he was waiting to be lit at just the right angle. Tony wears velour shirts and dark trousers and definitely no hat.

The angle of the light was pronounced satisfactory.

"Clear the set! We're ready for Miss Clare." The call went out from one assistant to another, down a row of people wearing black clothes and headphones.

I was thinking, Miss Clare? Could this be the luckiest day of my life? Am I about to see Dana Clare close up? Dana Clare is my favorite actress. She's only fifteen, and she has already made two movies. One was *Romeo and Juliet*, and the other one was a really funny story about a girl who gets lost up a chimney into space.

Sure enough, Dana Clare stepped out of her trailer and came striding over to the bakery door. She was dressed in regular jeans and a jacket, but I could tell she was wearing movie makeup. She and the director had a little pow-wow with their heads close together, and then she nodded and said, "Okay, Steven." He stepped back beside the big camera that was mounted on a complicated apparatus with wheels.

"Quiet on the set. Thank you. Rolling camera. And action . . ." Dana fumbled in her jacket pocket for a scrap of paper. Then she looked at the bakery and back down to the paper, comparing. She crumpled the paper into a ball and tossed it behind her onto the road. Litterbug. Then she reached for the brass handle on the bakery door.

"Cut!" called the director. "That was fine, Dana. Let's do it again for good luck. Could someone put the paper back?"

An assistant jumped forward with a fresh scrap and scooped up the other one from the street.

"Uh, Steven," said Dana. "Shouldn't there be something on the paper? I mean, it's blank."

"Sure, Dana, write anything you want." The same assistant gave her a pencil. She scribbled for a moment and then handed it back.

"Quiet on the set, please."

That was my cue. I decided I was going to be in the movie with Dana Clare. I leapt the curb and was at her side in one silent motion.

Just as the boss said "Action!" I turned and waved at the camera. Dana's fingers fiddled with her pocket while I grinned and did a dance of happiness. I was maybe eight inches away from her. In fact, my flapping hands made her hair shift a little, like there was a breeze. She glanced up to see where it came from. She looked at the bakery. She looked at me. She looked at the paper. She crumpled the paper and this time let it drop out of her hand onto the sidewalk beside her shoe. She reached for the bakery door.

"Cut. Print. Beautiful moment of confusion, Dana. Ten-minute break."

I waited until everyone was moving before I picked up the paper. I watched Dana Clare saunter back to her trailer. My heart was doing somersaults. I tried to peek in the window, but the blinds were pulled down so I could only see her shadow moving across the light.

I nearly got crushed by the lighting guys as they maneuvered the equipment to set up the shot inside the bakery. I decided to keep moving. As I strolled along the block, I uncurled the ball of paper. I had to lay it down on the sidewalk so that I could see it to read. It said: *Vesuvio Bakery. Dana Clare.*

I smoothed it out and held it flat between

my palms. I put it carefully into my back pocket without creasing the edges. Then I did a cartwheel, right in the middle of Prince Street. And then I danced four blocks before I stopped for breath at the corner of Broadway.

8 • *Candy Land*

Dean & Deluca was right across the street. Dean & Deluca is the fanciest food store in the world. They have 234 different kinds of cheeses, from 106 different countries. I know because I asked one time. We usually just buy cream cheese to go on bagels and sometimes a couple of stinky ones if my mother is having a party. I don't know who really needs 234 kinds of cheese, but they have them—just in case.

They also have a special person who comes in to arrange the fruits and vegetables. My mom told us that this person is not a fruit expert but an artist, who knows how to enhance the beauty of one thing by placing it next to a certain other thing. I guess it does take a special eye to do that with potatoes and apples.

Since I was so close, I thought I might as well go in and have a peek at the candy.

The candy is displayed in huge glass canisters, so big that even the salesperson needs two hands to take the lids off. The gleaming jars hold chocolate-covered raisins, gum balls, sour balls, Jordan Almonds, Smarties, peppermints, toffees, and jelly beans in every color. When we go with my mother, she'll let us have a treat about every third visit. She is very strict about sugar. Jane always picks bubblegum-flavored jelly beans, and I always get malted milk balls.

I stood next to the jar of malted milk balls, wondering how I could lift the lid without making it clink or disappear. There was a lady in a pink coat, waiting her turn, and a man with a mustache beside her.

But the clerk was listening to another woman. She was wearing a white fur coat and complaining about something she bought last week.

"I got two pounds of chocolate rosebuds, and they didn't seem fresh to me."

"Well, madam, we'd be glad to replace them, but you need to bring in the candy you think was stale."

"Oh, well, I ate them. I forced myself to eat them. But they weren't fresh. They didn't seem fresh to me."

"I'm sorry, but unless you return the goods, we have no way of knowing . . ."

"You can take my word for it. They weren't fresh. I would like a refund."

"But you ate them!" The clerk was trying not to seem too exasperated, but I could tell it was not long until blastoff. I could also tell that this Fur Lady customer, with her flippy hair, was the type of person who usually gets her way. I stuck my tongue way out at her. The other people waiting were getting restless.

"She's going to eat the salesgirl in a minute," the Pink Coat Lady murmured to her friend. I stifled my giggle.

I gave up my dream of free malted milk balls. I was turning to leave when a teenaged boy bumped against Pink Coat, and I saw his hand slide into her pocket and come out with a pink wallet. He was down the aisle faster than I could even see his face. But I saw the wart on his thumb and a rope bracelet.

"Hey!" I shouted and started to run after him.

"What's going on?" I could hear the voices behind me. I raced to the door, but the guy must have had wings. He was nowhere. I went back inside, with my heart pumping in my throat.

The people had heard me shout and seen

the guy running, but since they couldn't see me and I couldn't tell them what had happened, they were all just standing around doing nothing. At least the Fur Coat Lady had given up and moved on. But the Pink Coat Lady didn't even know yet that she'd been robbed. She was ordering dried apricots and the clerk was filling a bag! She was going to get to the cash register and be totally humiliated. I couldn't bear to watch.

I left the store, burning with frustration. Okay, I admit I swiped a snack today, and I even admit it was fun. But actually putting your hand into someone's pocket, that's just rude and bad.

My mother has tried to teach me that no problem is too great to solve, but I honestly couldn't figure out what to do. Here I was, with super-powers, and that's what stopped me from saving the day! If I were visible, I could have been a witness and given a description and maybe they would have caught the guy. Or then again, maybe I just would have been in trouble for not being in school.

I felt terrible. I was about to steal candy and

then this happened, and there was nothing I could do about it. I jammed my foot against the curb. And then again. I stood there kicking the concrete for about five minutes, imagining the robber's rear end was under my sneaker.

I wanted to tell somebody what I'd seen. If only I could have tripped the guy, I wouldn't feel like such a loser.

I wanted to tell my mom, but I knew I couldn't. I had to tell Hubert. Oh, my God, I told Hubert I would be back in an hour! It was way longer than an hour! He would be going nuts! And what if he didn't get my backpack from Alyssa? What if she found the powder and stuff?

I started to gallop. Suddenly it seemed urgent that I get back to school.

Ms. Shephard was sitting at her desk, scratching her ear, as though nothing had happened at all. The clock in the front hall said 11:34. My class has Early Lunch. I headed for the cafeteria.

9 • *Voice Tricks*

Sure enough, Hubert was sitting at Table Six with Charley and Josh. His plate was nearly empty, and he was stirring leftover tortellini with his fork in a definite "I'm finished" motion.

I stood beside the disposal chute, anticipating his next move. As he tipped the plate, I gently grabbed his wrist. He screamed. I mean, a boy scream. More like a squawk. Everyone in the cafeteria stopped moving to look at Hubert, just as he figured out it was me.

"Ooops!" he said with a silly laugh. "I thought I saw a dead rat in the chute."

"Ooooooh gross!" the chorus jeered.

Hubert yanked his arm away from me and scraped his plate. He stomped up the stairs.

"I'm sorry, Hubert." I tried to pat his shoulder, but he was going too fast.

"Hubert, I didn't mean to scare you."

He stopped short and I crashed into him.

"You didn't scare me. You just made everybody look at me." His voice was tight. "And where have you been, anyway? You said an hour, Billie, and it's been over two!"

"Did you get my pack?"

"Well, I know where it is, anyway," he muttered. "Alyssa said she's not giving it back unless she gives it to you, and she says you owe her for not snitching that you're skipping school, and she says when your mom gets back after lunch you are going to be dead meat."

He didn't even try to look at me. He was staring at the floor like it was hard to keep talking.

"Hubert—"

"Shhh!"

Noise behind me in the stairwell signaled kids coming up from the cafeteria. Hubert bent over to tie his shoelace as an excuse for standing there like a goof. We waited for half the third grade to go by, with me crushed against the railing and Hubert retying his lace about four times. It gave me time to think.

"Okay, Hubert, I've got a new plan. I just have to figure out where to do it."

"What's your idea, Billie? Not anything stupid, I hope, because I'm not really having fun today, even if you are. And where were you, anyway?"

"Oh, Hubert, so much happened. I'll tell you later, but right now, we have to do something. Come on." I put my fingers around his wrist, as gently as I could, and led him to the main hall.

Our timing was perfect. My mother was shepherding the second-graders through the front doors. I felt a little rush of happiness to see her. She's not exactly pretty, but she does have a nice smile. It makes her eyes crinkle up and look shiny.

"We have to make her hear me, Hubert, even though she doesn't see me. If she hears my voice, she'll think I'm here."

The bell rang for the afternoon classes.

All the kids in my mother's group were heading up the stairs to their room. The library is in the basement, next to the cafeteria, so I figured she would be heading downstairs.

I put my lips right next to Hubert's ear, like a mosquito.

"As soon as she moves, start calling to me."

My mother turned toward the library stairs without glancing our way.

"Hey, Billie, wait up!" cried Hubert, in a ridiculous voice.

"You can't catch me, Hubert!" I called, as if I'd ducked around the corner. "You'll be late, Hubert, you better hurry!"

"Hubert!" My mother scolded as she turned around. "Tell that daughter of mine to calm down. You both know better than to shout in the hallways."

"Yes, ma'am," said Hubert eagerly. He was so proud of our performance.

I followed him to class. I had to get my backpack. We were a few minutes late. Ms. Maloney, the sub, already had everybody seated on the carpet for a meeting. Hubert squeezed in next to Sarah, and I stood by the door, leaning against the frame.

Ms. Maloney borrowed a Mets baseball cap from David C. to put in the middle of the rug. She had cut up a class list and now put all the slips of paper into the hat.

"Okay, kids," she said, "Ms. McPhee asked me to do this today because she knows you'll need all week to work on your Small World assignments. This is the big moment. Each of you will have a turn to pull a name from the hat and read it aloud. The person whose name is on the paper will then tell us his or her country. Then that person will pick the next name. I know that Ms. McPhee suggested that you should each have a second choice ready in case your first choice gets taken by someone else. I can't listen to any disputes. This is the system that Ms. McPhee recommended, leaving it to plain old chance. If there's a problem, you'll have to talk to her about it. We'll have our first research period right after the selections. Does everybody understand?"

They all murmured yes. I wasn't worried about not choosing today. I was pretty sure that nobody else would think of Liechtenstein. It doesn't exactly jump off the map.

"Okay, David, since it's your hat, you choose the first name."

David drew Renée, and Renée picked France

because she went there last summer with her aunt. Renée drew Josh, and Josh picked the Dominican Republic because he loves baseball and that's where the best players come from. Then Josh drew Alyssa. She tilted her head to one side and coyly made her announcement.

"I have chosen to do my Small World project about China," said Alyssa.

I gagged. Everyone was looking at Hubert, but of course Hubert was looking at the floor.

Ms. Maloney was sharp enough to know that something was wrong with this picture.

"Why did you choose China, Alyssa?" she asked.

"Well," said Alyssa earnestly, "China is a very important country because it has the largest population in the world. I think it's going to play a big part in the next ten years of international politics, and I'd like to find out more about it."

"We'll look forward to your report, Alyssa. Thank you." Alyssa sat down with her eyes flashing in triumph. She reached for the name slips and warbled out, "Charley," while I stood there wanting to spit. Hubert looked in my direction from across the circle and slowly crossed his eyes.

Charley picked Australia. Nina picked Greenland. Hubert picked Bali. He said later he didn't have a second choice ready. Bali is the name of a place his mother says she'd like to run away to sometimes, and it just popped into his head.

10 • Story Time

I was so mad I left the room. I trailed down the stairs to the library, punching the wall along the way.

Even though she couldn't help me, I sort of wanted to be near my mother. I sat in the corner next to the window, with my feet scrunched up under me. I wanted to strangle Alyssa. How can someone always be so mean?

My mother was browsing in the picture book section. She was wearing the blue plaid shirt that I like. Better than her striped one, anyway.

After a couple of minutes, I heard the giggles and whispers of the kindergarten kids. It was Jane's class coming for Reading Time. My mother was going to read them a story.

It took a few minutes to get everyone settled on the green mat. I could only see my mother's back. Jane was curled up next to her. The other kids were all watching with complete attention.

They call her Ms. Stoner, and they think that everything she says is true and smart. No wonder she likes this job so much.

She held up the book to show them the first picture. It was *Millions of Cats*. I used to love that book. It's almost like poetry, the way "hundreds and thousands and millions of cats" gets repeated in a chant. I loved the way my mother's voice sounded saying it over and over. I closed my eyes and listened. I could remember snuggling up to her, just like Jane. Lying on the navy corduroy couch at home, begging her to read it again.

What if I don't come back? What if I really don't? The thought entered my head and stayed there, gnawing. I wanted to run over and hug my mother. I wanted to put my head in her lap and let her stroke my hair. I silently apologized for every rude thing I'd ever said to her.

And what if I do come back? I wouldn't be able to tell her what happened. It would be a secret from her forever. My mother wouldn't really see all of me from then on. My life would be more and more away from her as I got older. And what about her? Do I ever see her? Or is she invisible because she's just my mom? I was feeling dizzy from all this thinking. I admit, my eyes got hot and my nose was stinging, I was trying so hard not to cry.

I put my palms flat across my eyes and breathed slowly. I suppose if I waited long enough, the powder would wear off, but how long would it be? There must be a solution. I would go and get Hubert. Together we would find a cure! I would get the antidote for my condition. Like an explorer in the jungle with a snakebite.

I opened my eyes and caught my breath. Alyssa was leaning against the table. She slammed down a stack of books about China. She pulled out a chair with a scraping sound, dropping my backpack, as well as her own, onto the floor between us. She sat next to me with a thump.

My mother turned around and shot her a warning glare. Alyssa made a snooty face behind her back. I had to sit on my hands so I wouldn't smack her. Then she flipped open the top-most book and started to write on her note-pad. She looked back and forth between her page and the book and kept steadily writing. It took only a minute to figure out that she was copying, word for word, everything in the book. I could tell she wasn't even reading the words. She probably didn't know what she'd just written.

Suddenly I was determined to get revenge.

I couldn't wait to tell Hubert, but I was trapped by Alyssa and her pile of books. I sat there, as quietly as I could, trying to come up with a plan. This was one bad guy I intended to catch!

The bell rang in the distance of stairs and corridors. My mother ushered the little kids into the hallway. Jane held on for an extra minute, but my mother managed to peel her arms away and send her off with the others.

Hubert poked his nose around the corner. He was coming to look for me. I tried to think how I could let him know I was there. He saw my pack at the same moment that he saw Alyssa. She looked at him with disdain.

"Excuse me, Bertie," she sneered. "I just have to reshelve these books on China." She stood up and pushed past him. I quickly leaned over and poked his shoulder.

"Aah!" he cried.

"What?" Alyssa stopped to stare at him.

"You did a very bad thing," said Hubert. He

was showing me he could stand up for himself.

"You did a very bad thing," mimicked Alyssa. "Ooooh. You scare me. What are you going to do to me, Bertie? Blow a bubble in my face?" She fake-laughed over to the card file.

My mother chose that moment to come around the stacks.

"Alyssa Morgan, I've had enough of your noise today. Hubert, is everything all right?"

"Sure." His eyes skipped around the library, wanting to warn me, but my mother had spotted my backpack.

"Isn't that Billie's?" she asked, picking it up. It couldn't be anyone else's. Not with a huge STONER in liquid-gold marker on the back pocket and twelve keychains hanging from the zipper.

"Uh, yeah."

"Hey," interrupted Alyssa. "I was looking after that for Billie." She stepped closer and reached past Hubert for it.

"I haven't seen anything of Billie today," said my mother in that jolly voice she uses when she thinks she's missing something. She was still holding on to the backpack. My keychain collection jingled slightly.

"I haven't seen much of her myself," said Hubert. I wanted to kick him. "But I'll take her pack, Ms. Stoner. I'll be seeing her any minute."

"You haven't seen her," said Alyssa to my mother, "because she's not here. She hasn't been here all day."

11 • Phone Call

I didn't wait to see what my mother's face looked like. I was out the door before my next breath.

"Hey, Alyssa!" I called from the hallway, "Sarah's looking for you."

I popped my head back in.

"There she is now," said my mother. Alyssa's story was too unlikely to consider. "Shouting again. Hubert, when you catch up to her, please tell her I'd like to see her."

"Yes, ma'am."

Alyssa was shocked to hear my voice, and she started directly toward me to investigate. Hubert tried to follow, armed with a new sense of bravery.

"Hubert?" My mother handed him my backpack. "And Hubert? It's not right to chew gum in school. It's distracting for the other students."

"Sorry," he mumbled. He took his gum out and wrapped it in a piece of paper. She smiled at him and went back to her desk.

I was waiting by the door.

"Come to the phone booth," I muttered as we watched Alyssa's rear end wobble up the stairs. "It is time for desperate measures."

The public telephone is in an old closet opposite the front door in the main hall.

"Come in quick," I hissed, trying to drag him in beside me without Ms. Shephard craning her neck to notice. He closed the door. We were a snug fit.

"Hubert! You were brilliant. You kept your

cool and you saved the day!" I was feeling kind of fond of him. "And thank you for getting my backpack! Now give it to me. We have to find the person who belongs to the little bag."

"What do you mean?"

"I mean, I want to reappear. I'm going to phone the number that was in the bag. Jody Greengard. Maybe there's a cure."

"Good idea, Billie. Why didn't you think of that earlier?"

"Oh, shoot, if I'm holding it, it disappears. You're going to have to dig it out, Hubert. See? Being invisible has its disadvantages. I think I better come back."

"I have to admit, I miss your freckles."

I tried to punch him, but we were so crowded, I cracked my knuckles against the wall instead.

He pulled out the satin bag. He opened the zipper and it didn't even stick. He poked at the pots and tubes.

"Well, they don't look too thrilling. Which one did you use, Billie?"

I nudged the compact.

"What do you think this one does?" He picked out the biggest pot and started to unscrew the lid.

"Hubert! Don't! We have no idea what could happen! What if it's shrinking cream or it makes hair grow all over your hands?"

He put it back with great care. He slid his fingers around inside until he found the cards. The number for Jody Greengard was on the membership card to Dr. Dingo's Science Club.

"Okay, Billie, just phone."

"I need a quarter."

He sighed a sigh of enormous suffering, but he stuck a quarter in the slot.

I dialed. The phone rang twice and got picked up with a clatter at the other end.

"Hello?" The person was whispering.

"Hello?" I said back. "Is this Jody Greengard?"

"Who's calling?"

"Um, I have something that I think is yours. I found a bag in the park."

"You found it! That's so cool!" She stopped whispering, and suddenly I could tell she was a teenager. "When can I get it?"

"Well, there's a problem," I said. "I'm invisible."

The silence on the other end was complete. I thought the line was cut.

"Hello?" I said.

Hubert was poking me.

"Who is it?" he whispered. "Is it a wizard or something?"

I stepped on his foot. The telephone is the one place where everyone is invisible. I could be talking to anyone, a girl with green hair or a brain surgeon.

"Hello? Did you hear me? I'm invisible and I want to get uninvisible. I mean, I want to reappear."

"Wow," said Jody. "It works! I never tried it on a person before! This is totally cool. I've got to see you. I mean, you've got to come here immediately. I have a broken ankle and I can't go anywhere so you'll have to come here. I was whispering in case you were my teacher. I wanted to sound like I'm in pain. I must examine you. I broke my ankle when I was looking for my bag. How long have you been invisible? Oh, thank you for finding the bag. When can you come?"

I was thinking, when can you stop talking?

"The thing is," I said, ignoring Hubert's pokes. "The thing I'm wondering is, can you make me come back? Do you have a cure for the powder?"

"How old are you?"

"Nearly eleven."

"So you're ten. Wow. I made my dog disappear and come back, and about a hundred bugs, but I didn't know if it would work on people."

My heart took a dive. I could feel it flopping around in my stomach.

"Look," I said, summoning my bravery, "if I come to your house now, can you help me?"

"I hope so," she said, without a lot of conviction. "Yeah, but you better come as soon as you can, before my mother gets home from work. She will kill, I mean KILL me if she finds out that the powder works and I'm a genius."

"Is the address the same as on this membership card?"

"Uh-huh."

"I'm on my way." I hung up and turned to Hubert. I'm glad he couldn't see me because I was about to cry. My nose was stinging again.

12 • Subway

Well?" said Hubert.

I took a deep breath.

"We have to go uptown, Hubert. This girl, Jody, she's a teenager and she invented this stuff and she thinks she might be able to help but we have to go. Right now."

"I can't go, Billie. That's hooky. Why do I have to go?"

"Hubert, do you seriously think I'm going uptown by myself?"

That got him.

He opened the door to the telephone closet and closed it again quickly. We both should have been in class at this time of day. Ms. Shephard would be sure to say something. She might even be efficient enough to accompany Hubert back to the room. We had to think of a way to get out of the school without her seeing us. Seeing him.

I stepped into the hall, leaving Hubert hidden. I crab-walked past Ms. Shephard with my eyes crossed and my head lolling to one side. I went along to the empty music room and slipped inside. Then I started to laugh like a lunatic and slammed the door five times in a row. Ms. Shephard was out of her seat in no time. I walked right past her as she went to find the culprit.

Hubert and I were out the front door like professional cat burglars.

I held Hubert's hand while we walked to the subway. I never would have done that on a normal day, but somehow today it was okay.

Jody's address was 26 West Eighty-fourth Street. We figured out that it must be close to the Museum of Natural History because the subway stop there is Eighty-first Street. And we knew from our City Study class in the third grade that the numbers uptown start at Central Park and go west and east from there. So number 26 must be within a block or two of the park.

We headed for the C train. We've both been to the museum enough times to know that much.

At the entrance to the subway, my stomach clenched. My legs felt as if they hadn't worked in a long time. I was so glad to have Hubert with me. And even though he didn't say anything, he held my hand a little tighter, so I knew he was nervous, too, about going into the subway without grown-ups for the first time.

We started down the stairs. The smell of pee and the smell of the chemical they use to wash away the pee were fighting for first place.

There was a homeless man sitting on a crushed cardboard box on the bottom step, his neck and face wrapped in a rainbow-colored scarf. A coffee can stood by his feet with a few pennies in it.

Hubert let go of me and fumbled for his bus pass as he went a few steps ahead. I pulled two nickels out of my jeans pocket and tossed them into the man's can. They landed with a tinny chime. The man grunted in alarm and looked around him wildly, clutching at his shabby jacket. Maybe I shouldn't have scared him, but it was kind of funny, too.

Hubert showed his pass to the token clerk with a practiced wave. His dad usually brings him to school on the subway. With my knees scraping the grimy concrete, I ducked under the turnstile, just as the train was pulling into the station.

Hubert got a seat right away, next to the doors. I didn't want to sit, in case someone sat on top of me, so I stood up and held on to the pole.

I liked that subway ride. Because no one could see me, I felt completely safe. It was like a science fiction movie, and I was the alien. Hubert was trying to act cool, but he was sweating with fear. He thought someone would notice that a ten-year-old should not be riding around in the middle of the day. But no one even glanced at him. The other riders were either reading the *Post* or gazing off into space. Grown-ups pretend that someone's briefcase

or bottom pressing into them is a totally normal thing. Lucky for me, I could really stare
for a change.

At the Forty-second Street stop, a lot more people crowded on. I had to wiggle a bit to avoid getting squished, but I had a close-up view of several chest pockets and bosoms and hair beads and chins. Inspected closely, chins do not have much to recommend them.

What if I suddenly popped back right now? I thought. All these people would be astounded. Oh, please let that not happen!

Getting off the train at Eighty-first Street was more of a problem than I had planned for. I was stuck in the middle of the car, and I couldn't just say "Getting off, please," like a regular person.

Hubert held the door, which kept trying to close. I had to push a bit, and I accidentally stepped on one man's shoe. He glared at Hubert and said, "Oh, excuuuuse me," in a really mean way.

I poked Hubert to let him know I was there. I shoved through just as the door was closing. I feel so sorry for people who have to do that every day. It was making me sweat, just doing it once.

13 • One Last Fling

Getting back to the street and the sunshine made us both feel better. We stood facing Central Park, with the Museum of Natural History looming up on our right. That meant that we had to walk away from the museum to get to Eighty-fourth Street. It only took us a few minutes to figure it all out. That's one good thing about a city with numbers for streets; you only have to know how to count.

The park was waiting for spring. The trees were full of teeny green spots, about to burst open. The grass was looking like grass instead of muddy hay. The sun seemed brighter here than it had downtown, maybe because it had all that nature to reflect on. I felt slightly giddy and happy.

A horse-drawn carriage paused at the corner. One of those fancy things for tourists, with plastic roses looped across the canopy.

An idea flashed into my head. It felt like my last chance.

"Hubert," I ordered, "stand right here. Do not move an inch. I'll be right back."

One second later I was hauling myself up the side of the coach. I slipped into the seat behind the driver. Across from me were a man and a woman wearing matching fedoras.

The driver clicked his tongue, and away we went. We clopped down the road with taxis and cars zooming past. The spring air breezed around us. As we rode along beside the park, I felt like a royal person surveying my lands.

"Oh, Pete," the lady sighed, and put her head on the man's shoulder, making her silly hat go crooked.

Silently, I begged them not to start smooching right in front of me.

I turned around and knelt on the seat so I could see the horse. He was old and white with barnacles on his knees and a red ribbon braided into his tail. At the stoplight, I hopped down, wishing I had time to go around the whole park.

I raced back to Hubert, who was standing like a statue on the corner.

"Okay," I said, a bit out of breath. "Here I am."

"Where did you go?" he whined. "You left me alone!"

I hesitated. I knew he would disapprove.

"Oh, my God, Billie, you didn't pee in the street, did you?"

I started to laugh and couldn't stop. I had to stuff my fist into my mouth so I wouldn't make noise. Finally, I pulled myself together.

"Let's go. We've got important business."

Number 26 West Eighty-fourth Street was a three-story house. A New York brownstone, except that the bricks were painted pale gray and the shutters were black. There were red window boxes under every window with pointy green shoots sticking up.

Hubert said point-blank that he was not going in.

"I got you this far safely. I'll wait outside. If there's a lunatic in there, I might have to go for

help. And don't bother to butter me up. I'm staying here."

He parked himself across the street, leaning against a hydrant.

I climbed the steps and lifted the wooden knocker, which was shaped like a coiled snake. It sounded like a drum when it struck.

I heard a bird singing. I heard a siren far away. No one came to the door. I realized the knocker was just for show. I pushed a button I hadn't seen before.

Suddenly there was a fanfare of yips and

barks on the other side of the door. A blare of static came from the intercom, and then a crackly voice.

"Hello?"

"Hello?" I said. "This is Billie Stoner. I have your bag."

"Come in and come up the stairs. Come all the way up to the top." The handle clicked and the door swung open.

I looked across the street at Hubert. I waved, but of course he couldn't see me.

A floppy white dog with black freckles on his rump and a lopsided eye patch jumped up on me and started to lick. It felt good that someone knew exactly where I was.

14 • *Jody*

After the sparkle of the day outside on the stoop, it was dim in the hall, like switching the light off. But the dog wasn't waiting for my eyes to get adjusted. She slid across the polished floor with her nails clattering, heading for the wooden staircase.

I followed my leader and started to climb, rubbing my fingers along the fancy carved railing. There were wooden pineapples on the end posts. The second-floor landing had wallpaper with flowers the size of basketballs. All the doors were closed so I couldn't sneak a peek.

"Keep coming!" a voice called from above. The dog was way ahead of me. I started up the second flight. The stairs were creaking like crazy, announcing my every step. I felt like a ghost in a haunted house.

On the third floor, the bathroom door was slightly open, but all I could see was an old-fashioned marble sink with shining faucets and rows of gray tile like old teeth.

"You're almost here." The voice encouraged me upward.

My legs were aching. In our building, we have an elevator. Imagine if Jane had to climb all these stairs!

But when I got to the top, the climb was definitely worth it. The stairway opened straight into one big room. It wasn't a musty, creepy attic because sunlight burst through skylights in the ceiling, making a bright and wonderful greenhouse. At least, it was partly a greenhouse, with ivy and herbs and flowers growing in pots along all the windowsills.

It was partly a laboratory, too, with rubber hoses and test tubes and a Bunsen burner. Liquids of different colors sat in glass beakers on a table under the skylight, casting rainbows on the walls. The sloped ceiling came down almost to my shoulders. The only place a person could stand up straight was in the middle of the room.

The floor was a maze of electric train tracks going between and under all the furniture. Where there weren't tracks or chairs or table legs, there were piles and piles and piles of books, like a miniature city of wacky skyscrapers.

It was the most beautiful room I ever saw.

But I didn't take it all in at first, because first there was Jody. She was standing at the top of the stairs, leaning on a crutch and grinning down at me, just as if she could see me.

"Hey!" she said, when I reached the next-to-last stair. "Stop right there!" Her mouth was so full of braces that she looked like she'd eaten one of her railway tracks. Her left foot was in a walking cast.

"Can I have my bag?"

I put down my backpack and groped inside. The bag was invisible when I tried to hand it to her, so I put it down on the top step. She leaned over to scoop it up.

"Okay," she said. "Stay there. Don't move. I'm going to sit down. You come up and sit down anywhere, and I'm going to guess where you are. I'll give you a tip. The outer edges of the stairs don't creak."

She hobbled away and sat in a rolling office chair across the room, propping her crutch against the slanted wall. The dog flopped down across her feet. I guessed that Jody was about fifteen, but she wasn't much taller than I am. She had eyes the color of black coffee, and her hair was so silky and thin that her ears stuck right out from under. She was wearing a wild shirt with shiny polka dots on it and maybe her father's corduroy pants, scrunched together at the waist with a purple tie. It was so weird, it was cool.

I crept up the sides of the stairs and crouched near the table where her chemistry stuff was set up.

"Watch out behind you!" she shouted, just as my backside hit a stack of books and sent them sprawling across the floor.

"How did you know which way was behind me?"

She laughed, making a sound like a broken blender.

"I cheated," she said. "First, I watched Pepper sniffing to see where you were. And whichever way you turned, you were going to knock something over. It's a simple magician's trick: Distract the audience and pretend to know more than you do."

That last line made me feel uneasy.

"I never met a magician in real life," I said, "but I'm sure you're very nice and you probably know more than you think." Like how to cure me, I was praying.

"I'm a total loser at school," said Jody casually, as if she were dismissing a dull book. "Everybody hates me. I talk too much and I'm a nerd. They don't get me. I'm smarter than they are, by a mile, and I have a mouth full of metal." She smiled at me. "In case you haven't noticed."

"I like your metal mouth," I said. "It makes you shine."

"Oh, you should hear what they call me at school. Tinsel-Teeth. Appliance-Head. Fence-Face."

I laughed, but I was embarrassed, too. I knew that if Hubert, or better yet, Alyssa, had braces, I would get very creative with names.

"Anyway, I don't care about them. I don't even care that I'm a total disappointment to my mother. My brain alarms her. She just wants me to go shopping with her. And I just hope she finds the right thing to wear when I'm accepting the Nobel Prize."

It was comforting to know that even a genius teenager, with years of experience, did not have a perfect relationship with her mother. Maybe nobody does.

But I was here for a reason.

"I'm sure you will win the Nobel Prize," I said. "You'll be famous and rich and travel all over the world. And I hope it's for discovering a foolproof potion for making invisible things reappear."

15 • Gum Quest

She got the point.

"Okay," she said. "Let's get on with it. I hope I remember everything. I know the one thing I'm short on is masticated chicle. But maybe you can help me with that."

"What?"

"Masticated chicle. That's my fancy name for chewed-up gum. It's actually the gum juice that I use, but the gum has to get chewed first. Enough to release the juice but not so much that the flavor disappears."

I was thinking two things: Eww, gross—and Hubert.

Jody was rattling on.

"See, I can't chew the gum myself because of my braces. And I can't really store the juice for very long because fresh seems to work best. There used to be these two kids, twins, who lived next door. Cleo and Kimberly. They had great jaws. But they moved to Pittsfield. So now I have to scramble for my supply. We need about a cupful. Of gum juice."

"You mean right now? Before we can do anything?" She didn't seem to realize that I was about to scream.

"Yep."

"Well, lucky for you . . . I mean, lucky for me, I happen to have a champion gum-chewer downstairs, waiting for me across the street.

He can blow a bubble inside a bubble inside a bubble!"

"That's a very handy skill," said Jody in mock admiration.

"I'll go get him," I said.

"Well," said Jody. "We also don't have any gum."

When I stepped outside, the street seemed like a surprise. Just that it was still there, quietly being a street, holding Jody and this crazy house right in its middle.

Hubert was looking at his watch, probably counting the seconds until he went to the police station. He didn't see the door open and close, and he certainly didn't see me approaching.

"Hey," I said from a few feet away. He moaned.

"Oh, no! Billie! What happened? Why aren't you here?"

I told him the whole story. When I came to the gum part, his face turned from a stormy scowl to beaming sunshine.

"That's easy!" he said. "I'm the master chewer of all time! Did you tell her?"

"Yes, you show-off. And now's your chance to put your skills to good use."

"Let's go."

We set out down Eighty-fourth Street, away from Central Park and toward Columbus Avenue, figuring that's where the stores would be. There was a little newspaper kiosk one block down that had magazines and candy and lots of gum, right there on the street.

Hubert bought three packs of Banana Bubbalot and I stole another eleven packs, some banana and the rest cinnamon. It felt bad to keep stealing, especially after seeing the pickpocket, but we didn't have a choice. I knew I would have to fix things later. Hubert was embarrassed, but he couldn't help his dopey little smirk when I stuffed his pockets full of gum.

"Okay, big shot, start chewing." We began our mission.

Something nudged my leg. I looked down to see a puppy sniffing at me. His head rubbed against me like an invitation to play. His owner was trying to get a newspaper out of the box with one hand while he held the pup's leash with the other. I knelt down to stroke him. When I looked up at Hubert, he was watching in alarm. The owner couldn't figure out why his pet was sniffing at nothing with such pleasure. Hubert quickly leaned over to pat the puppy.

"Nice dog," he said. "I guess he can smell my gum." The man tugged on the leash, and the puppy moved on to a hydrant.

16 • *Master Chewer*

We sat on a bench outside the ice cream store, tipping our faces into the sun and chewing intently.

"Do you think I can still get a sunburn?" I wondered aloud. Hubert didn't answer.

"We don't have anywhere to put the gum," he said after a minute.

"Wait here a sec," I said.

I stood up and poked my head into the ice cream store. There were stacks of paper cups behind the counter. I promised myself it was the last time I would do this.

I waited for the lady to get busy wiping tables, and then I ducked under the little counter hatch and swiped a couple of cups.

Back outside, Hubert was looking around in dismay.

"I'm here," I said, sliding onto the bench next to him.

"I don't like the way you keep disappearing," said Hubert. I laughed.

"What were you doing?"

I put the cups in his lap to answer the question.

"You've got to stop this, Billie," he scolded. He was bent over, pretending to scratch his leg, while he talked to me so that no one would think he was a loony.

"Yeah, yeah, I know. It's almost over. I hope. Now get chewing! And don't fool around with any of your tricks."

We peeled off the paper, chomped into the gum, and worked it into soft, juicy wads. Hubert can fit seven jumbo pieces of Bubbalot in his mouth at once, so his cup filled up faster than mine. We wandered back to Jody's house, chewing all the way, pausing only to spit the next ready wad into a cup. Making the change from banana to cinnamon was a taste challenge, but Hubert put one banana aside for his last piece, just to look forward to.

"Won't you come in with me this time,

Hubert? Please, please, pretty please? With Bubbalot on top?"

"I'll think about it." He was getting better at looking in the right place when he looked at me. He stood on the stoop, pretending he hadn't decided, but I could tell he was too curious not to come in, now that he knew we wouldn't be locked in the broom closet and used for soup ingredients.

Jody's voice crackled through the intercom and Pepper's barking greeted us as we opened the door. We headed up the stairs like regular visitors, with me in front and Hubert behind, groaning about how many steps there were. But he shut up quickly when he saw the lab and the chemicals and the train.

"Hey there!" Jody smiled at Hubert, her braces glinting under the skylight.

"Hey," he said back, already a fan.

"Still chewing, huh? How much have you got?" We showed her our cups. Mine was only half full, but Hubert was almost done.

My jaws were aching, like I'd just spent

the afternoon smiling at my gram's friends.

"I have to take a break," I said. "Hubert, you can fill mine." I sat down in the rolling chair and rubbed my cheeks.

"I got everything together while you were out. I hope I remember everything," Jody said.

Hubert kept on stoically chewing. He was playing with Jody's satin bag, taking out the makeup and lining up the pots on the table.

"What does all this other stuff do, anyway?" Hubert asked as he unwrapped another piece of gum. "Is it all magic?"

"These are scientific experiments," Jody scolded. "Magic is for babies. I am a scientist and an inventor."

"Sorry."

"That clear lipstick makes everything you eat taste like strawberry pie, which just happens to be my favorite food."

"That might be the greatest invention I ever heard of," I said. "Except for Hubert, it would have to be Banana Bubbalot!"

"Yeah," said Hubert, "and I sure could use it. My mother is the worst cook."

"And this lipstick . . ." Jody rolled out the tube of coral that I had first looked at in my own bathroom. "Well, maybe you should just try it and see."

17 • *Rhyme Scheme*

I took it from her, and it disappeared. But I could feel the slim case, to roll it in and out.

"It's not going to, you know, do any permanent damage, is it?"

"Just try it."

"Billie, don't," said Hubert.

Jody flashed me a silver smile. "I promise, you will not turn into a werewolf."

I rolled the lipstick over my lips, expecting a tingle or a flavor. But nothing happened. Jody was looking my way with an expectant grin.

"Nothing's changed a single bit. There must be something wrong with it. Did you give me the right one? Are you teasing me for fun?"

The words tumbled out like a high-speed tape.

"Oops." I covered my mouth as if I'd burped at the lunch table.

Jody shook with laughter. Hubert snorted. How did I fall for this?

"You mean that now I speak in rhyme? And this will happen all the time? What about when I'm at school? They'll all think that I'm a fool!" I had horrible visions of trying to present my Small World Project in verse. Alyssa's smirk flashed in front of my eyes.

"Fix me up without delay! Give me something right away!" I glared at Jody, wishing she could see my fury.

"This one's easy," Jody reassured me. "Just wipe it off with a tissue and then gargle with vinegar."

She heaved a gallon jug of Grand Union white vinegar from under her table. I wiped my lips raw on the sleeve of my sweatshirt and then took a swig. I wanted to vomit at once. I swilled it around for maybe four seconds and then spat it out into the saucer that Jody was offering.

"I better not be talking in rhyme . . ." I tested the cure. They both applauded.

"That was funny," said Hubert. "You're pretty smart, Jody. Now what do we do with all this gum?" He handed her two full cups.

"Let's get going," said Jody. "You'll have to carry all this stuff. I'll need my hands for the railings." She gave him back the gum, along with a canister of talcum powder; a box of dog biscuits; a net bag of something dried and black and twisty, like fungus; and two test tubes from a tray on her lab table.

"When I did Pepper in the kitchen sink, she kept jumping out, and there was such a mess afterward, you wouldn't believe. I think we'd better do this in the bathtub."

"Wait a minute," I said. "I have to take a bath?"

"Of course you have to take a bath. What did you think?"

"I guess I didn't really think," I mumbled. Hubert was the color of cherry bubblegum, he was so embarrassed.

"Come on," said Jody, limping to the stairs. "We haven't got all day. My mother is going to be home before you know it."

"Oh, shoot," said Hubert, looking at his watch while trying to keep the cups upright, "it's really late, Billie. You better get moving."

I didn't have much of a choice, did I?

"Hubert, you have to wait up here," I ordered, taking his armload of ingredients, which vanished immediately.

Jody went down the stairs sideways, like a baby, and she only stepped on Pepper's tail once.

18 • *Chowder Bath*

As with most great creations of science, from the planet Earth to the human body, this formula is mostly water."

She turned on the hot-water tap with a flick of her wrist. The water poured into the tub, splashing on the marble veins, making them look alive. She dumped the contents of both test tubes under the flow. The water turned yellow immediately. She crumbled bits of the fungus and watched as they absorbed water and doubled in size. She shook in some talcum powder and then some more.

"I've never made a big batch before." She gave me a weak smile. "I'm not really sure of the quantities." She turned off the water.

"I guess it should be too strong rather than too weak. We wouldn't want you to look wispy or fuzzy or anything."

She put several dog biscuits on the floor.

"Help crush these," she commanded. Pepper was going crazy, but Jody kept shooing her back. I did a little dance in my sneakers, and Jody rolled her cast back and forth across the floor until the biscuits were chunks and crumbs. We scooped them up and dumped them into the tub. Pepper licked the traces off the tiles.

"Now the gum." She took fistfuls of gum wads and squeezed them over the mixture. Only the tiniest drops of juice dribbled out. Then she tossed the sticky lumps in with every

thing else. She rolled up a *Vogue* magazine that was lying on the floor and used it to stir with big, swishing turns.

"Oh, good, it's starting to thicken. Now take your clothes off."

I hesitated.

"Your body has to be completely covered," she said firmly. "You have to be immersed. You should have seen me doing Pepper. She kept slithering away from me, but she was invisible so she was hard to catch."

"So I really have to get into that and slop around? Like a snail in butter?"

Jody laughed.

"Uh-huh. Like a snail in butter. That's a good one." She saluted and limped into the hall. "I'll be waiting outside," she called as she closed the door.

I looked down at the tub full of chowder. I looked down at where I should be. I pushed off my sneakers without untying them, thinking how that drives my mother crazy. I peeled off my socks.

I unstrapped my watch and tucked it into the pocket of my jeans. I could see its face for the first time since this morning. Yikes! It was after two o'clock. Time was galloping by. Sweatshirt, jeans, and underwear reappeared as they flew from my hands into a rumpled pile beside the toilet.

It was so weird to be naked in a stranger's house with Hubert creaking around in the attic above me.

As much as I did not want to, I dipped my left foot into the soup. It was warm. I stepped in with my other foot. It was like standing in the squishy kind of mud that lives at the bottoms of lakes.

"Five, four, three, two, one . . ." I sat down. I smeared the disgusting stuff on my face, my shoulders, my stomach. I flipped over and wiggled around, just to make sure. I opened my eyes, hoping hard that I would be there.

"It's not working!" I wailed.

19 • Try, Try Again

The door swung open. Jody's brown eyes peered around it. Pepper poked his nose in.

"Oh!" remembered Jody. "It has to be dark! You know, 'in order to come out of the darkness, the light must first be extinguished . . .' "

I wondered if that was a real quote from somebody.

Jody lurched across the room in her cast and pulled down the window shade. She flipped the switch on the wall as she went back out the door, leaving me in the kind of dark that is inside a theater just before the show begins. You can see the shapes of people all around you, but nobody has a face.

I sloshed around for about a minute, wondering how long it might take. I closed my eyes. I let my head go all the way under and came up again quickly. I rubbed the muck into my hair like shampoo. The combined smells of dog biscuits and talcum powder and fungus were beginning to get to me. I plugged my nose. I started to wipe the biggest chunks off my knees, when I realized that I could sort of see my knees!

"I can see my knees! I can sort of see my knees! It's working! Everything's coming back!" I stood up and did a slippery jig.

The door flew open with a crash.

"Get out of here!" I shouted at Jody. "You don't have to see *everything!*"

"Ooops, sorry," she said, retreating to the hallway. "It's just so cool, so cool, so totally cool."

I heard Hubert's voice calling from the attic, muffled but excited.

"Yeah," Jody shouted up to him, "it's working!"

"Hey, Billie," she called to me. "You can take a shower and rinse it all off now."

Hubert's feet clunked down the stairs. They were standing there in the hall, waiting for me to appear.

I pulled the shower curtain closed and

turned on the tap. I could hear Jody yammering away. Well, I guess she deserved to be a little pleased with herself.

The shower was delicious after the bath. I used the Mango Shower Gel that was on the bath sill and rinsed away every gloopy drop of dog biscuit and gum. I washed my fabulous, reawakened hair and let the water pour over me like a waterfall on a Hawaiian hillside.

But, as I scrubbed my wonderful, visible legs and my lovely, reappeared arms, I realized that something wasn't quite right. Most of me was back, pale and freckly as usual. But my hands and feet were still a bit vague. I can't think of another way to describe it except that they weren't really all there. As if the felt pen ran out of ink before the picture was finished.

I dried off and got dressed, with my heart as heavy as it had ever been. My hair was still drippy and tangled so I swooped it up in a towel turban. I didn't bother to put on my sneakers.

I opened the door to the hall to face my friends. Pepper put her paws right up and sniffed me all over. Jody actually jumped up and down, with her cast thudding against the wooden floor. Hubert was grinning like he just won first prize at the Computer Fair.

Then I held up my hands. For a second, they didn't get it. Then they focused on the faintness of my fingers.

"Oops," said Jody.

20 • Halfway There

My feet are the same," I said, lifting one and then the other for them to inspect.

"Oh, no!" cried Hubert. "What are we going to do now? Everybody'll notice if she doesn't have hands!"

Jody's face was screwed up in concentration. She looked like an old gnome.

"Don't panic," she said. "There has to be a solution. There is a solution to every problem."

"That's what my mother says," I said.

"Your mother is right," said Jody. "Turn on the tap in the sink. The cold tap."

We all pushed into the bathroom together, eager to try anything. The cold water rushed into the marble basin, and Jody shoved my hands under and held them there. The water got icier the longer it ran and, if anything, my hands faded slightly more.

"So much for that idea," whined Hubert. "Do you know it's nearly two-thirty, Billie? We couldn't get back to school on time if we had a helicopter. We are in so much trouble we might as well kill ourselves."

"Too bad I haven't invented a flight potion," giggled Jody as she dried my hands on an eensy guest towel. "Don't worry; I have another idea." She reached into the bathroom cupboard and took out a hair dryer, shaped like a violet machine gun. I could tell that Hubert was getting more upset by the second.

Jody plugged in the hair dryer and fiddled with the settings.

"This is going to be hot, Billie," she said,

pointing the weapon right at me. The hot air blew on my hands, and Jody waved it back and forth for even coverage. Sure enough, only a couple of minutes went by before we could see a change. Bit by bit, my hands were looking more substantial.

"Hubert, stop bobbling about like that." He was making me nervous. "Go get my backpack. As soon as my hands are done, we're leaving. I can wear my socks and do my feet at home. Come on! We're late!" Hubert scuttled off upstairs while Jody kept the hot air blowing at me.

"Let me ask you something while Hubert's not here to protest," I said. "I need a teeny-tiny bit of the vanishing powder."

Jody looked at me with her skimpy eyebrows scrunched low over her eyes.

"I swear, I will not use it on any living thing," I vowed, "but I need it to perform an urgent act of revenge."

"Revenge?" That hooked her.

"If it works, I'll call you and tell you all about it. I still need to figure out the details, but I promise you it is entirely deserved."

A grown-up would have insisted on hearing a specific plan, but Jody was cool.

"You take over here," said Jody, handing me the hair dryer. She lurched upstairs just as Hubert was coming down. Pepper went crazy for a minute, scrambling after Jody and then doubling back to make sure Hubert made it safely. By the time Jody was back, so were my hands. I turned off the hair dryer. I pulled my socks on over my half feet. I tied my sneakers.

Jody handed me a film canister, which I slid into the zipper pocket of my pack.

I gave her a hug.

"Thanks," I said. "You saved me."

"Thank you," said Jody, "for being my first human subject."

No need to linger or get mushy. Hubert and I had a serious deadline.

21 • Deep Doo-doo

Even though we were way late for school, we'd been uptown for less than two hours. And so much had happened.

It made me think of Ms. McPhee's introduction to history this year. She said that time has a way of stretching and shrinking, depending on how you're using it. If you're eating ice cream, five minutes can fly by. But if you're holding your finger over a candle, five minutes is longer than you can bear.

What I hadn't figured out yet was whether the trip had been blissful or unbearable. Just extraordinary, I guess.

Hubert and I jogged to the subway.

At the top of the stairs, there was a raggedy old woman doing a shuffling dance step and tapping a tambourine. Her hat lay upside down on the ground, holding a dollar bill. I reached into my pocket to pull out my money, and the lady's face went all happy and crinkly.

"Oh, bless you, honey, bless you." She had a whistle on her *s*'s.

"Wait a minute, Big Spender," said Hubert, "you're not invisible anymore. You have to pay to get on the train."

The old dancer lady was watching me carefully. I counted the money in my pocket. I was short by forty-five cents.

"I'm sorry, ma'am," I said. My voice got small. "I don't even have enough to get home."

She bent over and took the dollar bill out of her hat.

"You go on home, honey," she said, handing it to me.

I bought my token and put it in the slot. Hubert waved his pass. We stood close together

on the platform. It felt different this time, now that people could see me. But there were also a lot of other kids and teenagers on the platform. That was good for camouflage, but it also meant that school was already out.

When the train came, we stood up and held on to the pole nearest the door. It felt more like we were going somewhere.

"My mother is going to be nuts," said Hubert at the Fifty-ninth Street station.

"My mother is going to be double nuts," I

said. I checked my watch. Fiftieth Street. Forty-second Street. Hubert checked his watch.

Nobody knew that I'd been invisible an hour ago. Nobody knew that my mother was probably faint with distress at that very moment. We were all just riding along, minding our own business.

Thirty-fourth Street. We were members of a tribe of anonymous New Yorkers, chugging along together. We didn't have to explain ourselves to anybody. Hubert checked his watch again. Twenty-third Street. Fourteenth Street.

"Maybe we better think of an explanation," I said. "Don't you think we need a story?" But Hubert was past rational thought.

We got off the train at West Fourth Street and hurtled up the stairway to the sidewalk above.

When we turned the corner onto Bleecker Street, my feet stopped moving before my body, so I stumbled in shock at what I saw.

Police! There was a police car parked at an odd angle next to the curb in front of the school. I could see my mother talking to an officer on the steps, and another one was interviewing Hubert's father.

"We are in deep doo-doo, Hubert."

22 • The Story

We ducked back into the entrance of the Banana Republic clothing store and tried to spy through the display window. There was a crowd of kids leaning against the wall of the school, pretending not to notice what was going on but with their ears flapping from so much eavesdropping. I spotted Renée and Charley and Josh from our class. And Alyssa, of course, whispering to Sarah behind her hand.

My watch said twenty minutes to four. We were twenty-five minutes late. I wondered when my mother had figured out I wasn't there.

"What are we going to do?" moaned Hubert. He was really upset.

"I think we'll have to rely on mother-love to get us out of this one. Leave it to me." I galloped out of the store and across the street.

"Mom!" I waved and hollered as I ran. "Mom! Mom! It's okay! We're okay!"

Jane saw me first. She was standing on the steps, and she heard me and started to shriek. Nobody could figure out why she was shrieking until she pointed, and by then I was right there.

Jane threw herself at me from the top step and I staggered, but I held on to her. Hubert came toddling along, and his dad grabbed him. My mother burst into tears and fell on me. Jane got trapped in the middle, and we were all a big, huggy lump for a few minutes. When my mother's sobbing got quieter, the police officer interrupted.

"Er, excuse me; I'm very happy to see that the children are safe. We just need some information for our report. Would you tell me where you've been?"

I could tell from the way he looked at me that he was a father and probably a nosy one.

He held his pencil over his notebook and he held his eyebrow arched over his eye at the same time.

I took a slow breath.

"Hubert is really the hero," I started. I thought maybe the ideas would catch up if I could stretch out the words a bit. "Yep, it was Hubert who really saved the day."

Hubert was staring at me with wide, horrified eyes.

"Just before the last class, um, just before science, Hubert noticed that my backpack was, um, that my backpack had disappeared." I might as well start with the truth.

"And then from the window, he saw someone wearing it and leaving the school."

"Would this person belong to the school community?" asked the officer.

"Was it someone you recognized, Hubert?" asked my mother.

"Uh, he wasn't sure," I said quickly. Hubert was responding too slowly.

"That's why he grabbed me and said we should follow the person."

"Why didn't you inform an adult?" asked the officer.

"You should have told Ms. McPhee immediately," said my mother.

"Ms. McPhee is sick today, Ms. Stoner," said Hubert.

"Oh, yes," said my mother.

"Yeah, and that dopey substitute probably wouldn't have believed us," I said. My mother glared at my disrespect, but she was still holding on to me with helpless gratitude, so I kept going.

"There was no time to lose. We saw my backpack disappearing up Sixth Avenue so we just went after it. We knew we'd be okay because we were together, and we are both very responsible." I thought I'd better slip that in.

"How did you get your belongings back?" asked the officer.

"Did you confront the thief? Did you know who it was?" asked my mother.

Hubert's eyes were now scrunched up with curiosity. He was waiting to hear what happened next. The policeman was making scratches in his pad, but he paused to wait for my answer.

"Well, you know, it was the weirdest thing." I played for time. "At first we could see the person in front of us, and then, poof, like magic, we couldn't see the person anymore. We thought maybe he'd gone into the subway and then, and then . . ."

"And then, there was the backpack," said Hubert helpfully. "It was just there, leaning against the front of the newsstand. The guy must have gone through it and realized it was totally worthless."

"Hey, thanks a lot," I said.

"Well, you certainly gave your parents and teachers a fright," said the officer.

"Next time, tell a grown-up," said my mother. "No matter what."

Her eyes were getting wet again. I could tell she'd had a rough time. I thought about how much I'd missed her this afternoon, even though I was sitting in the library five feet away and just happened to be invisible. So for her, having me disappear and not knowing I was all right, well, no wonder she looked awful.

"Okay," I said.

"Sorry," said Hubert.

Jane kept squeezing me and patting me. I crouched down and gave her an Eskimo kiss, nose to nose.

I couldn't believe we were getting away so easily. We shook hands with both officers and waved when they drove off down Bleecker Street.

Hubert and I didn't have even a second alone. Our parents whisked us off in opposite directions.

23 • Caught

As soon as I could after we got home, I borrowed my mother's hair dryer and went into the bathroom. I peeled off my socks and shoes and blew hot air on my feet. They looked normal pretty quickly except for the toes. The toes didn't quite make it. I would have to keep my socks on for a couple of years.

Then I had to style my hair and make it look

all poofy, so my mother and Jane wouldn't wonder what I'd been doing. Even though she didn't
say anything, my mother was watching me with
serious interest.

All through supper, my mother alternated
between smothering me with kisses and scold-
ing me over and over for behaving so thought-
lessly. I don't know which was worse. I had to
answer twelve thousand questions from Jane
about the backpack thief. I told her he had a
wart on his thumb and was wearing a rope
bracelet.

When I was finally lying in bed, my mother
came in. She is just tall enough so that her face
pokes through the slats of the guardrail on the
upper bunk.

"Billie," she whispered, shining her lovely
smile on me. "I just wanted to tell you again
that I love you. I'm glad you got your backpack
back today, even though you should have asked
a grown-up for help. I'm proud that you and
Hubert stuck together."

I lay there, letting her words lull me.

"But there is still one thing I'm curious about. . . ."

I felt a warning prickle all over my body.

"I've been wondering . . . I didn't see you to-day . . . Mr. Belenky said you weren't in chorus. Alyssa said you weren't in class, even though I heard you shouting in the halls a couple of times. . . . What actually happened?"

She looked at me with those smart eyes, and I knew I was caught.

"Mom," I said. I looked up at the ceiling for guidance.

I decided to take a chance.

"Mom, here's what happened. I found a pot of magic powder, but I didn't know it was magic. When I put it on, I disappeared. I called the person whose name was with the powder and she said to come over so she could cure me. Hubert came, too, as my gallant protector. And it's a good thing he did because we needed chewed-up gum to make the potion. And you know how good Hubert is with gum, right?"

I looked at my mother to make sure she was following me. She cleared her throat.

"Billie, you have a fertile imagination."

"It's the truth, Mom, but if you don't believe me, I understand. It's a bit of a wild story. The important thing is, I got home safely, and so did Hubert, and nobody got hurt and I was very responsible and I learned a lot about the world and I love you and I even love Jane, and you'll never know how glad I am to be home."

I held my breath. Would telling the fantastic truth work? She gazed at me with soppy eyes and then tucked my duvet around my shoulders and said good night.

24 • *Revenge*

Hubert and I were famous for a couple of days at school. We told everyone the same dumb story, and then we said we didn't want to talk about it anymore.

On Tuesday, Ms. McPhee was back, with a red nose. She posted a schedule of our Small World presentations on the bulletin board. I was on the list for next Monday, so I had a whole extra weekend to finish. Hubert was supposed to do his on Friday. He was getting a little nervous about the talking-to-the-whole-class part, but I told him to practice in front of the mirror.

It was Alyssa's turn that I was interested in and, lucky for me, it was one of the first. On Thursday, Charley was doing Australia, and Alyssa was doing China.

Phase One of my plan was that I had to be in the classroom before anyone else on Thursday. I gave Jane a piggyback ride most of the way to school so that we wouldn't have to crawl at her pace. For once, my mother acted like a storybook mother and said good-bye conveniently quickly.

My revenge was simple, and the plan was easily executed. I had decided not to tell Hubert because he might have stopped me.

As the morning ticked by, I got giddy with anticipation. Finally, it was Small World time. Charley was first. His talk was pretty good. He spent a little too much time discussing the damage a dingo dog can do to a human limb, but aside from that, it was interesting.

As he was finishing, I watched Alyssa. During question time, she went to her cubby to get her material. I clasped my hands together to stop myself from clapping with glee. She turned to Ms. McPhee and started to whine.

"My folder's not here. I put it here and it's not here."

"Don't fuss, Alyssa. It's probably in someone else's cubby by mistake."

Alyssa's foot came up and stomped right

down again. Hubert looked at me suspiciously. I looked out the window.

Alyssa started to paw through other people's cubbies. Sarah hopped up to help her. After about fifteen tense and delightful minutes, the folder was discovered right where I'd "misplaced" it, on Ms. McPhee's desk, in the stack of homework files.

Alyssa snatched it from Ms. McPhee and flounced to center stage.

"My country is China," she announced. "China has more people than any other country." She flipped open her book.

I had to sit on my hands.

Her eyebrows pinched together. She scrambled through a few pages.

(All I had to do was to find Alyssa's work folder in her messy cubby and open it to the pages she had copied from the encyclopedia. I sprinkled the tiniest bit of powder over the writing, hardly even dust. Just enough to melt away the ink without affecting the paper or the binder. In fact, I could still see fragments of words here and there, but nowhere a complete sentence.)

She looked up in complete disbelief.

"My research is all ruined!" she cried, holding up the binder for everyone to see. "All my writing is gone!"

"Well, then, Alyssa," said Ms. McPhee soothingly, "try telling us what you know about your country, without your notes. What is the weather like, for instance? What sort of food do all those people eat? What are the conditions for women in Chinese culture?"

Alyssa's gray face, her bugging-out eyes, her violet neck, her look of complete stupidity . . . this was all I needed to feel that Hubert was avenged.

I grinned at him. He slowly shook his head back and forth, and then he grinned, too.

"Excuse me, Ms. McPhee?" he said. "I could talk about China. I could, um, tell you lots of things that I know from my mom and dad."

Ms. McPhee rose to the occasion.

"Go ahead, Hubert. We'd love to hear your family's story. Alyssa, why don't you sit down and we'll discuss your problem later."

Oh, happy day.

Epilogue

This is the part of the story where all the loose ends get tied together into a neat little tassel.

A few weeks after the invisible day, I turned eleven.

One thing I got for my birthday was a diary.

I've been keeping a record of setting everything right.

First, when my mom took us into City Eden for an after-school snack, I pretended to find a dollar on the floor, and I gave it to the lady to pay for my banana and Doritos.

Second, I taped a subway token to a piece of cardboard and sent it to the Metropolitan Transit Authority to pay for my first ride uptown.

Third, I had to save a chunk of my allowance, which is only four dollars a week, before I could mail a ten-dollar bill to the newspaper kiosk on Columbus Avenue to pay for all the gum I stole. Who knows if mail gets delivered to a place like that, but I did my best.

The next time we went to the Museum of Natural History for a Family Excursion, I looked for the old lady with the tambourine, but she wasn't there, so she's still on my list.

When the movie starring Dana Clare was released, Hubert and I went, with our moms. The scene that I'm in is just before she finds out that the baker's sister is her real-life mother, who she's been searching for during the whole movie. I know it's the scene that I'm in because her hair ruffles a little bit while she's looking at the paper.

"That's me!" I whispered to Hubert. "That's my screen debut!"

"You deserve an Oscar," he whispered back.

And then Dana drops the paper on the ground beside her instead of tossing it onto the road. Hubert wouldn't believe me except that I showed him the paper. I keep it in my top drawer alongside the film canister holding the dregs of the vanishing powder. You never know when such a thing might come in handy.

Alyssa went crazy after her Small World big disaster. She even accused Sarah of sabotaging her project. Hubert and I rescued Sarah, and now she hangs out with us. She finally got some blue jeans.

I called Jody to tell her about my revenge on Alyssa, and she laughed for five minutes without stopping. Now we talk to each other on the phone at least once a week. I pretend it's someone from school, needing help with homework.

Another present for my eleventh birthday was that my mother gave me a key to our front door. Not to start using right away, she said, but after a little practice in "street smarts." So now we have a new routine for walking to school. I walk alone, a couple of blocks ahead of Jane and my mother, but still in their sight.

The first time I did it, I stopped to wait for a green light at the corner of LaGuardia Place. I looked back and waved at them. Jane waved wildly and then leaned over and wiggled her bottom in my direction, which is her idea of hilarious.

My mother didn't wave because her hands were jammed in her pockets. I know she wished she was next to me with her arm around my shoulder instead of trailing along behind. She had a shiny, fake smile on her face, trying to show how brave she is.

I blew her a kiss and walked the rest of the way to school without turning around. With my head up and my shoulders back, just like my mother taught me.